LEMONS ARE NOT RED

Laura Vaccaro Seeger

SQUARE FISH

A Neal Porter Book

ROARING BROOK PRESS

New York

Lemons are not

Lemon

Apples are RED

Carrots are not

Eggplants are PURPLE

Flamingos are not

Elephants are GRAY

Reindeer are not

Snowmen are WHITE

Grass is not

The sky is BLUE

The moon is not

SQUARE
FISH

Imprints of Macmillan Publishing Group, LLC
120 Broadway
New York, NY 10271
mackids.com

Square Fish and the Square Fish logo are trademarks of Macmillan and
are used by Roaring Brook Press under license from Macmillan.

Library of Congress Cataloging-in-Publication Data
Seeger, Laura Vaccaro. Lemons are not red / Laura Vaccaro Seeger.
p. cm.
"A Neal Porter book."
Summary: A simple story highlights such things as a yellow lemon, a pink flamingo, and a silver moon
in a visual game in which die-cut shapes fall on the correct color backgrounds.
1.   Color—Juvenile literature. [1. Color.] I. Title.
QC495.5.S44 2004   535.6 22   2005297028

Originally published in the United States by Henry Holt and Company
First Square Fish Edition: 2012
Square Fish logo designed by Filomena Tuosto

ISBN 978-1-59643-008-2 (Roaring Brook Press hardcover)
10 9 8 7

ISBN 978-1-59643-195-9 (Square Fish paperback)
21 23 25 27 29 30 28 26 24 22

LEXILE: NP